Turning Point

David Bell

Copyright!@2014
No portion of this book can
reproduced in any manor without the
author's permission. Skyline productions
Dream Scape
Technical Director Tony Bell

I turn

It was a night I'll never forget. It happened when I was about 11 or 12. I woke up in the middle of the night; I could hear voices in the air. A sudden tingling raced up my spine. I knew that they were tiny whispers; I could not make out any of the words being said. I was afraid to get out of bed thinking someone might hear me.

Is this day a turning point in my life? Will I be changed forever? Only God and destiny knows how this day will end up. I could tell that it was my parents speaking.

They did sound afraid. As much as I tried, I could only make out a few of their words. I knew that something had to be wrong, because my parents weren't in the habit of talking in the middle of the night.

My bedroom seems so empty and bare and I really feel alone. I clutched my blankets as if somehow they would protect me, from what I didn't even know. My blanket was very little comfort. Of course, my imagination was running wild. All kinds of wild ideas raced through my brain. It took me a long time to get to sleep.

When morning came, I was really tired; nightmares and confusing thoughts had kept me from getting any real sleep. During breakfast, nothing was the same. My parents were subdued, as if they were trying to protect or hide something from me. Why couldn't they tell me? I can be trusted. Then again, my parents weren't in the habit of sharing troubles with us kids.

They kept shooting nervous glances at each other. I tried to eat but, it wasn't easy. The hair stood up on the back of my neck. I was so scared and I didn't even know of what. I was afraid to ask them what was wrong. Whatever it was, I could tell they didn't want to talk about it. I rushed through my breakfast, not really knowing what I ate.

A tomb of strange silence surrounded me as I left the house. I was walking on egg shells. I welcomed the warm summer air. At least the sun was shining and I began to feel a little bit better. All my life I have been living in this little town. It is a quiet peaceful town; we have one high school, a movie theater two churches and a few businesses. There are two bars and a small Dairy Queen.

I would soon find out that this day would change all that. Nothing would ever be the same. Then it hit me like a brick, everything was different this morning. Neighbors' doors were closed, drapes were drawn, and nobody was standing or talking on the lawn. Fear crept back in.

I was afraid to look over my shoulder. I didn't feel safe just walking and I started running to school. Never before had school looked so inviting. I was actually glad to be there. The halls were full of students, some of them standing in bunches, others standing alone staring. They all had one thing in common, they all looked scared. Just as I was ready to ask my friend, what was going on the bell rang.

Even the teachers are different. They look down, instead of meeting anybody with their eyes. Instead of trying to help us, they seem to be just going through the motions. It is obvious they just wanted to get today over with.

When the school day was over, I ran to the store to buy a paper. I wanted to find out what was wrong. When I opened the paper, I froze in my tracks. I couldn't move I just stared. I'll never forget the headlines.

Two teenagers found slain.

I had put the paper down and started walking, as if I was in a trance. I must have walked for hours and it was becoming dark. I have to get home I thought, but I wasn't even sure where I was. I told myself I had to be calm. I started walking, hoping that I could figure out my way home. Nothing looked familiar.

Footsteps

I stopped, did I hear a noise? I was shaking. I had to get a grip on myself. I began to walk again, there was that noise again.

No mistaking it, yes, I definitely heard something.

Footsteps

My heart was beating loud. I should run, I should yell, but I couldn't do anything. I couldn't seem to make myself react. There they are again, footspets. They are getting closer. Not me, not me, I yell inside. I was filled with panic. I had to try to think.

Of all times, my mind was blank. The footsteps were getting closer and closer. I could even hear her breathing. Whoever it is, they don't sound friendly. I was afraid to look back. I was afraid of my own shadow. I just kept walking, trying to think of something, anything.

WHAM

A hand clutched my shoulder. The pain vibrated through my whole body. Trembling, I slowly started to turn around

Journey to the Sun

No matter how hard, no matter what temptation I face, I must not look back. But how could I help but to look back. My house below was fading out of sight. If you would've told me six months ago, I would be taking a trip to the Sun, I would have called you crazy.

It was six months ago. That's when it first began. A normal summer's day, as a matter of fact, it was a boring summer day. Or so I thought at the time. I was at the school ground like I had been countless times before, when I noticed a bright flash of light over the Western skies.

A cold chill raced through my spine. It wasn't long before I had forgotten that flash of light. It seemed like no one else noticed it. By the time I had made it home, I had forgotten all about that light. In my nightmares during the night, I could see that light again. It haunted me that night. During the night, when I walked to the kitchen for a drink of water, that flash of light followed me. It was there when I paced my bedroom floor. It interrupted me when I tried to write stories.

I know what you're thinking, but this is all true. That light wouldn't leave me alone. It flashed over and over again in my mind. I knew it had some kind of deep significance.

What it meant, I had no idea.

You won't believe how happy I was to see daylight. I tried to forget the night before. Under the warm summer sun, I put the previous incident out of my mind. I was actually successful in thinking that it never happened. But that was all a lie. Truth cannot be swept under the rug.

Everything seems different in the summer. Days are longer, nights are shorter. I had just finished my chores and I was ready to leave for home, when I noticed the western sky. A huge giant light lit up the sky. It was a lot more intense, brighter than before. I stared at it for minutes. I wondered if my eyes were deceiving me.

As quick as it appeared, it was gone. I blinked, spots were in my eyes. This time there was no mistake; there was a flash in the sky. Why hadn't anyone else seen it? Was it meant just for me?

It seems like the flashes are coming every day. Each day they last longer and are very intense. And that's how I ended up on the spaceship. Here I was, on my way. I knew it was a special mission. But the destination was unknown.

My house is getting smaller and smaller as we go higher into space. It was only two hours ago that I was in my bed, sleeping like a little baby. I was sleeping when the flashing lights woke me up. It lifted me out of my bed and put me in this rocket-ship.

Flying, rising in the sky, I was not quite sure of my destiny. The seat I am sitting on is made out of a cushion of light. I have one tiny window that I can see out of it. Looking out it, I can see my progress. I think I am the only person on this ship.

I'm not sure how the ship works. I am scared, but somehow the light reassures me. I know that I was picked for this mission for a special reason. I have decided to keep a journal. Maybe that is why I am on this ship. They wanted a writer to make the journey.

I drift in and out of sleep, and all I can see below me are clouds, thick white clouds. The sun looks larger and larger, and I wonder if that is our destination. The sun, the flash of light, it's all starting to make sense.

We are headed to the Sun, but why? As I look out my window, all I can see is the sun. I can no longer look. The sun hurts my eyes. Somehow the ship is protecting me from the heat.

I never realized the sun was so far away. When I can see the Earth, it looks smaller and smaller.

Darkness

I can't see anything.

Everything has become black. A cold chill runs through me. It is as if I am in a dark tunnel. Suddenly the light returns. It is no longer intense, it is soft and warm and it is calling to me. As I look out the window, it occurs to me that I am in the center of the sun. I closed my eyes. I will never forget this special journey. It seems like I can't get all of my emotions onto paper. I am trying to get everything down, so I won't forget.

I feel a slight vibrating feeling race through my body. It is sort of a tickling sensation. When I open my eyes, I am back, back in my house. I'm still in my bed. Perhaps, it was all a dream. My imagination is going wild. I look out my own window and wonder if it really happened.

Shaking looking out my bedroom window, a huge flash lights up the sky for a brief second. On the edge of my bed is a journal filled with scribbling. Was it real or not? I am positive I had gone to the sun. I will never know why.

As I watched the sky, a light fills my body for a few seconds. I wonder if someone is trying to tell me that our days on earth are numbered. I know that, I will never understand why I made that journey to the Sun. But I am glad I was chosen.

The attic

Often in life we look for places to hide. Real places or places in our mind. I find myself in a place of refuge. I have retreated to the attic. I love the attic. There is only one small window to the world. I rock in my chair looking out the window. I have found peace, and happiness.

I look out the window, like I have countless times before. If only I could tell them, let everyone know, that I am here. They seemed like they are only a few minutes away. Time has very little meaning. It is as if I am no longer controlled by the clock. Time has no meaning for me in the attic. I have so many emotions, I'm afraid to express them.

All I have left is memories and the joy of watching my family out this attic window. I am never to leave, never to understand, never to leave.

If you look close enough, my oldest daughter Marsha is standing by a tree. It doesn't seem that long ago that she was born. Time goes by so quickly. We had only been married a year when she was born. I was at work when I had received a phone call. It was a phone call that would change my life forever.

"Hurry" was all my wife could say.

Walking the hospital hallways, they seem darkened and forlorn. There was a constant chatter from the nurses at their desk. Quiet, I yelled inside my head. Down the hall there is an important event happening. I knew I would be a father soon.

I could hear my wife's cries. How I wanted to help her, reach out to her, and tell her how much I loved her. All I could do was wait, wait in torment. Waiting seemed to take an eternity. My nerves were on fire.

"You can come in."

There lying by my wife was a tiny little baby girl. A bundle of love, so tiny I was afraid to pick her up. She is 16 now, standing by that tree talking to a boy. I wonder if she misses me, misses her dad. Does she think of me at all?

As I sit in this attic, I torment myself with, should I have done this or that? I often wonder if I was a good parent. I have to say, I did my very best. Now it's up to my wife to bring them up. My wife is the greatest thing that ever has happened to me. She took a wandering, insecure boy and turned him into a man. I loved her hair and her smile. I loved everything about her. I do know that I told her I loved her, but I've never said it enough.

I did everything I could to show her that I loved her. I love you, I whisper while in the attic. Maybe the wind will catch my words and carry them to her. I know that she can't hear me. You see, I'm dead. My spirit lives on in the attic.

I rock in my chair, knowing that I can catch glimpses of my family out the window. I can hear them talking below me. Being in the attic is hard when they are away. When they are gone, it is just me, the attic and my memories. I will probably leave this attic someday, but not yet. I am not ready to let go of them.

I can hear my son Tony downstairs, talking about the day's soccer game. I wonder if he knew how much I loved to watch him play soccer. You often wonder, if your children understand, that you loved them. One thing is for sure, I should've told them when I had the chance.

Pam is my middle child. She is the different one and the independent one. It seems like I was always constantly yelling at her. I was always afraid something would happen to her.

I wanted to protect them, guard them from pain. I found out that you really can't protect them from the world. Often children have to make mistakes on their own.

I miss my wife so much. I miss talking to her, sharing with her. I am dreaming grand dreams of living with her. Sometimes foolish dreams, but we had a lot of fun. I miss her talking to me and often I am tempted to enter her dreams and talk to her.

Although I can hear and see them at times, it's not the same. I want to be with them. I want to make a difference in their lives. It's been 10 years since I have died. I think I'm ready to leave this attic.

Marsha has married, is living on her own and she has two children. She has really grown up and matured. Perhaps I didn't do such a bad job. Although I can hope, you're never sure how good of a parent you were.

Tony is going to college and is playing soccer. He is really tall. I can't believe how much he has grown. And you know what; he has even started writing a book. Maybe he wants to be a writer like I was.

Then there's Pam all that worry for nothing. She's working a good job and living with a friend of hers in their apartment.

I'm ready to leave this attic, because my wife has sold the house. As I look out the window I think that she can see me. I wave and blow her a kiss. She waves goodbye. I am free to leave. My spirit can go home.

The day after

There they are footsteps closer than before. There is a crackling of a branch only a few feet from me. Lying on the ground, I clutch the ground harder. I am trying not to breathe, not to move. The cold is almost unbearable, it is frigid.

In the distance I hear the barking of dogs, they sound so vicious. Are they hungry? Are they hungry for blood? Shadows of doubt surround me. Shadows lurk in my mind. Voices from the shadows are yelling back and forth. They are getting closer and my pounding heart may give me away.

All I can do is wait and see what happens. Will they find me? Flashes of light pierce the darkness. Humble soul, I am on the brink of insanity. My side hurts from jumping the fence and running. My hand clutches my injured side. Red oozing blood flows. It feels strange, as if it belongs to someone else.

Closing my eyes, the swamp disappears. I am in my bedroom on my bed. What I can't figure out is why there is blood on my bed. I keep having the same dream over and over again. It is as if I can't escape my dreams. Perhaps I have become trapped in my dreams, shackled by shame. I look at my bed and the blood is gone. I often wonder if I can tell what reality is. Perhaps my whole life is one big dream.

I look out my only window in my tiny one-room apartment. All I see is the bright blue sky. My apartment and what I call a trash heap is five floors up. Living life alone is a drag. No one should have to live like this. In the summertime heat is unbearable.

A fly is buzzing around my head, tormenting me. I closed my eyes and pictures of my former life sliced through my brain. How long has it been? It seems like 10,000 years, 10,000 boring years. So many things have happened. Those memories seem to flood my mind.

Journal, I read from my Journal. It all began on July 5, 1985.

July 5, the situation in the world is getting worse. If only I could change things. But like the rest of the world, I thought one person couldn't make a difference. I should have at least tried. I was working in my store, when the radio shouted out. I knew the world would never be the same. That's when I decided to keep this journal. Perhaps future generations can learn from our mistakes.

July 6, there is no music on the radio. It is filled with news reports and the fear of global warfare. Everyone's seems to continue their daily life. They act like humanity is invincible. It was as if everything is normal. I don't know why, but I closed my store early today. I checked out the shelter I had built underneath it.

It's unbelievable, but my store is built above the natural cavern. I constructed a stairway to the cavern.

July 7, I locked the doors on my store at noon, and put up the iron metal over the Windows. For now the outside world seems calm, but I know it won't last long. I can tell that war is coming. When I go back up to my store, I can hear people yelling. I lay on my floor and I can see people just walking back and forth as if they are lost. I am slowly taking food downstairs. Once I get everything stocked, I will destroy the stairway. The radio has just announced that war has been declared.

July 8 have to take time to rest. It takes a lot of work to carry the food down to the cavern. I have four lanterns lots of propane and a tiny propane oven. I have a lot of extra batteries for my radio in case the electricity goes off. As I closed my hidden trap door, I can hear the crowd outside breaking into my store. I was able to get everything I need below just in time.

July 9, I was awakened early by the ground shaking and a terrible rumbling. I can feel a searing heat. I turned on my generator and turned on the air conditioning. Still some of the heat makes it uncomfortable.

I think to myself it has begun. I sit in my chair and cry, screams of terror race through the air. I have a vent that goes to the outside so I can hear what's going on. After the screams there is complete silence. Is everyone dead?

It seems like the ground is always shaking and there is one explosion after another.

July 10th there are more and more explosions. I thought they had destroyed most of the atomic bombs. Finally silence, deadly silence. I turn on the radio to see if I can find out any news. There is nothing but static.

Have they managed to do it? Will I ever see another person again? Am I partially to blame for this war? After all, I never did anything to promote peace. Everyone should have demanded the destruction of all atomic bombs.

July 15, tears continue to penetrate my cavern. I suspect the world is like a giant oven. I am filled with despair. I can almost smell the burning of mankind. I try not to think about it. I would like to go upstairs but I am afraid of the radiation. The silence is driving me crazy.

I am thinking about looking outside. I don't want to live like this much longer.

September, 1 I have run out of fuel for my generator. I no longer have lights or electricity. My food is running low and someday I must go up. I wonder if there is anything left. The thought terrifies me.

September 4th I've given up trying to get anything on the radio. It is a hopeless cause. I think they did what they wanted. I worry that I might be the only person left alive.

December 27, I have decided this will be my final entry. The silence is unbearable. I have no food left, I must go up.

I throw my journal down. It seems so long ago that I had written it. Once I was outside, the animals have taken over the world. They are building houses and schools.

They have put me in the peoples' zoo. I am on display for all the animals to look at. They act like I am dangerous. Some of the young animals make fun of me. Would you have thought about trying to escape? I thought about it, but where would I go? What worries me, is that the animals are starting to build bombs. Will they face the same fate as mankind?

And the rain came

Where are we going my little one?

What are you doing little one? There seems to be one little loaf of bread that hasn't been eaten. Is there any hope left? This is a humble farm, but it is mine. It is all that I have left for my family. Not much of a legacy, but it comes from my heart.

I stand at the fence post and look at the field before me. What are you doing little one? I am looking at the field through childlike eyes, praying for rain. Nothing is growing, the ground is parched. Like a young baby, it needs nourishment.

There is not enough food to last us the winner. I look at the sky and there is not a cloud in sight. There is a small cabin behind me with my wife and kids inside. A small candle flickers in the window. They are depending on me.

It has been two years since I built this cabin and I'm beginning to think it was a big mistake. I lean on the fence post and can almost hear their voices. I know that they are counting on me to bring them through hard times.

I'm not sure we are going to make it. The field looks like a desert. The moon is smiling at me, but I don't smile back. It casts an eerie light over the field. I know that this isn't God's fault. It is just bad luck. Funny how some people take rain for granted.

I don't want to move again. Before we moved here I built a cabin. We have moved four times. I like it here. Besides, my wife is pregnant again. I have to give her credit, she never complains. She always supports me and has a smile on her face.

No matter what the hardship is, or how much work she has to do, she always says, God will provide. I am a lucky man to have met her and marry her. I waited till the children fell asleep before coming out to the field.

As I look at the moon, I recalled the journey that brought us here. It was a sad occasion leaving our old home behind. At our previous home, the fields had nothing left to give. We just couldn't stay there any longer. Behind the old house our oldest son is buried. He died of disease. When we left, I left part of my heart with him.

After he died, I no longer could get interested in the land or the house. It was a sad day when we loaded the wagon and headed to the new farm. I love our new home, I don't want to leave. I have a family that I have to think of. There has been four weeks of dust and not one drop of rain.

I am here standing at the fence waiting, praying, please

make it rain, if not for me, for my family. I had promised them that we would never move again.

And as if to answer my prayer, I feel a small drop of rain and my tears started falling. It begins to rain harder. It is bringing life to the crops. Best of all the rain has given the land life and I hope. Home, I have found my home and faith again.

The silent tomb

Quiet. I must be quiet. This is such a thrill. I have them all fooled. I am the great pretender. They tried everything. Nothing worked, never will. I am the greatest. I wouldn't talk. Why should I?

Tommy

That is what they call me but why should I reply? My home is Columbus, Ohio. But in reality I live within my mind. I live inside this protective shell. I'm a normal ten year old boy who has never talked. What is so great about talking? Seems like all they do is argue and shout. Who wants to live like that?

Nighttime.

Nighttime, is my favorite time. They leave me alone at night. I can live in my dreams at night. Everything is quiet and peaceful at night. They think I need friends. Who needs friends? Only weak people need friends.

I am the mighty warrior. I am the great cowboy dreamer. I don't need anyone. I have my stuffed animals and my dreams. Who could ask for anything more? I have a million thoughts, I'm not dumb. I just don't see any need to talk. No one I have met is worth talking to. They are the dumb ones. I am far superior. I have the advantage of listening, absorbing everything around me.

People are so two faced. They say one thing and then do the opposite. They say nice things to someone's face but say something else behind their back. They make me sick.

How can they act like that? Their voices sound so hollow, empty. I don't want to be like that. I wonder if they know I write stories and poems in the darkness of my room. I feel safe when I write. There is no hidden meaning in my words. I can be honest on paper. How many people can be honest when they talk?

I have true friends, the night, my stuffed animals and my dreams. They love me for who I am. No need to pretend. I even talk to them. I say actual real words. I love to stare at my ceiling at night. I like to drift off and think about the world. I don't care if I get much sleep. The night is fascinating. This is my silent tomb. Why should I ever speak? Give me just one good reason.

Finally I am able to fall asleep. Drifting through my make believe worlds. I wake up and the silence is deafening. The whole world seems quiet. My parents can't seem to talk. No birds are singing, even the wind is quiet.

I reject my silent tomb. I begin to speak. At first everyone looks sad. They are all looking at me. I stand before the world and tell my story. I knew I had to say something so the world could speak again. All of my words are honest.

As I stand on national television I have to decide what important words I can say. This may be the most important moment in history. Finally my first public words come out.

I love you. I love you.

Forbidden journey, awake

In truth our farm house is like others. There is nothing to set it apart. It is tiny, but nice, a few shingles on the side missing, but besides a few flaws, it is in good shape.

My parents seem to harbor a secret. They are always acting strange. They shun any neighbors. They are always warning us not to venture into the last field. What kind of secrets are hidden there in that field?

I am the quiet one in the family. They call me Robert. I love the outdoors. I don't like my name, but I tolerate it. I guess a lot of people aren't fond of their name. Perhaps it is our desire to be independent from our parents.

I am way different than my older sister Marsha. She acts like she knows everything even though she is only a year older than me. Girls are like that. They think boys don't know anything. She is always talking. She gets on my nerves. I try to ignore her. It isn't easy. But one thing we both do is try to behave around our parents.

My brother John is a year younger than me. A lot of people call us the staircase kids. I think it is a silly statement. John is very strong for his age. I am eleven. John is twice as strong as I am. I wonder why my siblings aren't curious as to what is behind the fence of the last field. Aren't they the least bit curious?

What is behind that fence? "Robert," my mom is calling me to eat. I hate being interrupted.

My brother and sister act like robots. They talk strange and always do what they are told. I feel alienated from my siblings. I wonder if I was adopted. I stare at my parents.

Parents?

They act more like royalty. I can't place a finger on it, but they are different than me.

Forbidden journey, pondering

After eating, I return to my bedroom. For some reason I have no toys. I don't complain because I don't know how to talk to my siblings. They don't seem to care that they don't have any toys. Nothing seems to bother them.

Since I have never been off the farm, it is hard to judge if our life is normal. Somehow I doubt that it is normal. My brother or sister hasn't been off the farm. They don't seem to care. Why am I so different? I want to know what the rest of the world is like.

I wish I could go to school. My parents don't send me to school. I am not sure why. Whenever I get the chance, I sneak to the edge of the road. And I watch the school bus drive by. I can hear the kids talking on it, and they seem to be just like me. Why can't I go to school?

One day I was even brave enough to visit the school. I spent the entire day behind a tree watching the kids play and talk. I was tempted to join them. But I knew that could lead to disaster. My sister and brother don't play with me, and they rarely talk to me.

Maybe I have some rare disease and my parents are trying to protect me. There was one day I made it all the way to the library and looked through some books. I found myself reading even though I've never learned to read.

With the short time I had, I read everything I could. After reading several books I realized that our family was different. My mind always returns to the field. I think the answer is hidden behind that field. There is no doubt in my mind; our strange existence is tied to that field.

You really can't call our place a farm, because we don't grow anything. We don't have any animals or even a pet. Matter of fact, I don't know how we live. My parents have never left the farm. They have no jobs.

We have no car, TV, or phone. I wonder where the food comes from. They never go to the store. Is it really food? On one trip to the library, I saw a cookbook and couldn't believe my eyes. There were pictures of food I had never seen.

There were apples, oranges and corn and green beans. Will I ever find out what's going on? As I go through the book, I don't recognize any of the food. I couldn't find any pictures of what we are eating. Trip after trip I visited the library. I stop going to the library. I stop going to the school, I was afraid that my parents would catch me. I am so confused. The books tell about dragons, castles, kings and I can't tell what is real. They show pictures of tall building and big cities.

The odd thing is that I can't recall anything about my past. What if I have no past? I fall to sleep, my questions put to rest for now.

Forbidden journey, morning sun.

In the distance I can hear a rooster as the sun wakes me. Wiping the cobwebs out of my eyes, I get dressed slowly. There is no hurry we never eat at a regular time. I close my bedroom door and head to the kitchen. No one else is here but I go ahead and eat.

No one is coming to eat and I'm starting to get worried. The front room is empty. I go to my parents' bedroom and knock lightly. There is no answer. I begin to pound on their door, still no answer. Something has to be wrong. I slowly open the door.

There is not a shred of furniture. I am shocked and afraid. Just who has been taking care of me? After checking my siblings' room, I notice the same thing. What is going on? Now I know that I am different.

With a strange feeling in the pit of my stomach, I look out the window at that fence. I suspect the answers are in the forbidden field.

Forbidden journey, answers

I know that today will change me forever; I am heading to that fence and field. Nothing can stop me. This day will change my life forever. My heart is in my throat. Step by step I get closer to my destiny. Am I really living? Perhaps this is a dream that has gone wrong.

Am I even human? I look like the other kids I saw at the school. I climb over the fence. So far it looks like any other empty field. All this time I had been warned to stay out of the field.

I am ready to turn around when I hear a strange noise. The ground begins to rumble and shake. I am not afraid. In front of me the earth begins to open. And a huge space ship starts to rise out of the ground.

I can see my parents and my brother and sister in the spaceship window. They are waving at me. I can hear them talking to me.

"You will be okay now; you are ready to join the rest of the humans."

The farm house and fence disappears and the ground closes back up. My real parents come running up to me.

"Where have you been," they asked.

"I've been on a journey," I answer.

I look at my classmates and they begin to clap. Perhaps I will win the short story contest. When I get home, my parents tell me not to go into the last field by the fence.

The other side

Temptations of the night haunted me. How I hated the night. It has been seven long years of torture, seven long years. I muse during the nights while others are able to sleep. I wish I could sleep. They don't know how lucky they are. But not I, sleep never comes easy.

I am a teacher at day and a monster at night. Daylight sees me as a gentle man teaching young children. During the night evil lurks. The nights are scary, if I can just live during the daylight hours only.

The day it first started, I can remember it so well. Who could ever forget? One of my students came up to me and said, "I'm going to cast a spell on you."

I paid little attention to him. I figured he was just trying to show off. For some reason I couldn't help him with anything. In fact, somehow I had become his mortal enemy. I just brushed aside his threat as pent up childhood anger. I left the school concerned that I had failed to reach him.

As I drove home I knew I couldn't help everyone. I entered my one room apartment. It was small, but nice. I sat in my favorite chair. I shouldn't let his anger bother me. But it did. I drifted off to sleep, a nervous sleep.

In a cold sweat I wake up. I felt a burning sensation in my skin. It started in my arms and began to spread.

It was so hot in my room, I thought I would die. I was stuck in my chair I could hear the students voice. Fear struck my heart. Was I still dreaming? No couldn't be. I was awake. I felt like it was my nerves. The burning sensation became stronger and stronger. It was as if my skin was burning from the inside out. I was on fire with pain. My body was splitting in two.

Standing in the room, facing me, was my exact double. I had become two people. My double looked evil. It was laughing at me, mocking my good behavior. "Do good person," it yelled at me.

It was off, ran away in a flash. I was too tired to move. At daybreak my double would return home and we became one person again. I knew that it was evil and doing bad things.

Seven years.
There is more evil and I was getting weaker. My double was killing me. I had to do something. But just what could I do? It may be way too late. Sometimes I am almost evil during the day. I have to something before it is too late.

Dark, it is starting again. I have become two people. My double is laughing at me. Laughing at me like hundreds of times before. My double is so evil it doesn't see me reach into my pocket.

It takes all my strength and resolve, I pull out my gun. I point it right at my doubles heart. I fire one round after another, I fire until my gun is empty.

It was dying, I felt like part of me was dying. For a while everything turns dark. Finally I am able to wake up. It had worked. My evil side was dead. I almost jumped for joy. For the first time in years I was able to sleep. I can't believe how good the morning sun looked.

A student from another class approaches me, "I'm

casting a spell on you."

When I looked around he had disappeared. Sweat began to pour from my head. The nighttime was only a few hours away. I walked out the school building as if I was in a trance.

Looking in a store window I could see an evil face laughing at me. Angrily I broke the window, and began to run. I ran until I couldn't run anymore. Wearily I sat on a rock to rest, when I could see my double coming to me.

He was wearing a devilish smile. I realize I cannot escape my double. I reached into my pocket and pulled out my gun. I pointed it at my head. A loud bang echoes through the air. I sat on my bed, the same dreams for over eight years now. Why can't I wake up? Why won't he leave me alone? I fall asleep. I was teaching school when a student came up to me

Castle in the night

There is that dream again. I will visit that special castle again. I never get tired of visiting it. Time stands still.

It's starting. The sun and its great glory begin a slow descent. I am watching the final last rays over the trees in the distance. It flickers over the rooftops. With one final faithful beam, it disappears out of sight.

A tiny cricket makes a sound as I jump out of my bed. Am I ready to leave the world behind? At my castle I can leave hunger and pain behind me. I forget about my bleak existence. I turn off my parents arguing. It is just me and the night. I am ready to visit my castle.

Slowly I drift away, waiting for my dream. A beautiful tranquility awakes. I have a dream that takes me away from reality, from the world. It is my dream and my dream alone. It is beginning, music enters my humble bedroom. I float around in a magical haze.

Soon I will be there. I am spinning.

My room is spinning; the music is getting louder and more demanding. Faster and faster I spin. My bedroom becomes one a giant blur. I have landed in magic land.

I am landing in a field of cotton with yellow clover. Aren't dreams great?

In the distance, not far away is my sparkling white castle. I bounce up and down, jumping. I wish that I could jump twenty feet high. When I jump the cotton catches me. I am having a joyous rebirth. I am walking the two foot wide red rose covered path.

I kick my heels and I am singing. It is such happy occasion. I feel like I'm on my way to Oz. I don't miss our tiny house or my parents. In this dream, I am very important. I must hurry or I will wake up before I reach the castle. I have had this dream many times and never made it to the castle.

I'm going to make it this time. It is only a few feet in front of me. I can't believe it. What good luck. The golden door stands before me. Slowly the oversized door opens. It looks dark inside. I enter my dream castle. Maybe I can leave my life behind.

Cold darkness surrounds me. I feel my way along the halls of the unknown. Does it lead to a room or does it go on forever? There is no light, no sounds and I wonder if this is a mistake.

The darkness is fools' gold. It mocks my feeble attempts to find my way. I know that this hallway will lead me to happiness. I hope that is what my dreams are about.

When I stop in the darkness I can hear my parents call.

"Where are you, where are you?"

I fall to the floor in frustration. Tears fill my eyes.

"I'm here. I'm here."

Just where am I? I have become trapped in my dreams. Trapped and I don't know how to get out. Will I ever escape this dream? The darkness closes in. Maybe the real world isn't so bad after all. I may never know. If I try, can I finally awake? I wish I could escape my dreams, but I can't. Will this be my final destiny? Do you my friends, live in your dreams?

Swamp creature of the night

Mosquitoes, what pesky little creatures, they never seem to tire. Even the flap of my nylon tent can't keep them out. Pesky little things, I can hear that strange sound again. It has happened every night at the same time for the last five years. Five years and no sign of the swamp creature, all I can hear are those strange sounds.

That lonely sound of his cry fills the night air. Five years of research and hunting and nothing to show for it. This misery, bad food and pain are all I have to show for five years of work. At first I thought it was a glorious adventure. I dreamed of being famous. I would be known as the person who had captured the fabled Swamp creature. I'm no closer to my goal after five long years.

Its cry is closer than ever. Constant rain, it seems like it is always raining. I often wonder if the rain will ever stop. The rain seems to make the air more muggy and the mosquitoes more vicious. Rain is everywhere, almost coming into my tent. This tent isn't very big but it is my home. I have a propane stove and a generator in back of the tent. I sleep during the day and stay up at nights.

For five years I have had very little contact with the outside world. Funny what five years of being alone can do to a person? It seems like reality and dreams mingled together. I have almost lost track of time. Five years seems more like 50 years.

The rain, but it never seems to stop. There is another hole in my tent. Surely the creature is getting closer. The sounds of his cry are closer. Maybe this will be the night. If not I am ready to give this up. There is no moon or stars. That means I won't be able to get a good picture of it. No one will believe me without any proof.

I look into the darkness, hope against hope. Lightning flashes through the sky and for a brief second of eternity, I see it. My heart is filled with excitement. I can't believe my eyes. I saw his furry face between two trees. I am not afraid. I'm just glad I wasn't wrong. He must have been close to seven feet tall.

All I could make out was his face; the flash was way too short. I get dressed quickly and grab my flashlight. Slowly, I head to the trees. Caution is my middle name. I search the area but I can't find anything.

I have decided to keep a journal. It will help me keep track of time. It is the only way I will be able to keep my sanity. When I am able to sleep, I see visions of monsters in my dreams.

June 14, and it's been one year since I saw a slight glimpse of the swamp monster. I decide not to leave; I have too much time invested. I think that it is watching me instead of me watching it. I have almost given up hope.

June 16, I can't seem to get organized any more. The swamp seems to be overpowering me. I tried to pretend that I'm still in control of my own life. Not sure if I'm crazy or not. I wonder what changes have happened in society since I have been gone.

July 1, I stay in bed for days at a time. I have lost my ambition to do anything. My tent is a complete mess. I can't get my mind off that one night I saw the creature. I feel tired and sick.

July 5, I've been having a lot of nightmares lately. Most of them are about the night I saw the creature. All the images in my head are distorted. I really believe that I am crazy. I'm not sure if I can go on much longer. I should go back. The creature in the swamp will not let me go back. I can't go without answers. Time seems to be standing still.

July 6, there is something in the air. The air seems to be different. Even the animals are acting strange. It is like a nervous element is in the air. Sometimes the sky is a bright orange. Maybe there is a storm somewhere. I haven't heard the cries of the creature at all today.

July 9, I must be getting sick.

I can't seem to stay warm even though the sun is burning bright. I shiver all day long and wrap myself with layers of clothing. My radio has quit working. I can't get anything on the radio. I get nothing, but static. In a moment of anger I throw my radio away. I have decided I will stay here only one more week.

July 20, I didn't leave. I heard the creature twice and did not have the courage or strength to leave. I can hardly walk and I am constantly cold. I see fewer and fewer animals. I feel like that I might die.

July 21, the creature is near. I can almost see it. But I am too weak to look for it. I can't seem to shake this illness. I'm not sure I have much longer to live. Not sure how long I can keep this journal. I can barely hold a pen.

August 4, I'm not sure if this is the correct date. I am writing this on my bed. This may be my last entry. The creature was just outside my tent last night. I could hear him breathing. I think it is waiting for me to die. I've got to rest now. Too tired to

August 15, I still can't believe it. That night when I thought I was going to die the Swamp creature entered my tent. I was too weak to even acknowledge its presence. It stood about 10 feet tall and was a solid black mass of fur.

I thought it was intent on killing me and then it picked

me up. It started carrying me. I drifted in and out of consciousness as he was carrying me, for what seemed like an eternity. At times I was delirious and would shout profanities and beat his chest.

Other times I just mumbled weakly. Finally after it made its way through the Swamp, it took me into a cave and laid me down. I was so ill, I passed out.

August 21, I'm trying to remember as much as I can. I know all of this seems too strange to be true, but it is. The Swamp creature or Igor, this is the name I gave it, has been feeding me with wild nuts, fish. He brings me water in a hollow log.

August 25, I am still weak, but I can feel my strength coming back. The creature resembles us humans, but he doesn't talk. We have built a mutual bond. I think the creature is studying me.

August 26, I think the creature recognizes his name. He goes out every night. I don't know where he goes. He never seems to sleep. As soon as I get my strength, I'll get back up going to follow it.

August 27, I followed Igor tonight, but I was tired and had to return my camp. I will try to follow it as soon as I can. Igor watches me as I write in my journal. He is trying to imitate me. For some reason he likes to hear me sing. I wonder if he is the only one of his kind.

August 29, I have given up trying to follow him. He is way too fast. I have realized I must head back to civilization.

September 1, I have decided not to tell anyone about the Swamp creature. He deserves to live in peace. I think I will miss him. We had become close friends. I hate to leave, but I don't belong here.

September 3, I think Igor knows that something is different today. He has an empty look on his face. I wish I could make him understand. My strength is back and I know I must leave today or I'll never be able to leave.

This is the saddest moment in my life. I look at him with sadness. I hugged him deeply. I walked toward the cave entrance. Slowly I turn. With a tear in my eye, I waved goodbye. He slowly lifts his arm. Is he crying? I swear I could see tears in his eyes.

September 6, I reached the edge of the swamp today. In front of me I could see the city. In the background I can hear his strange cry. I leave the swamp behind.

Journal footnote, I often dream of returning to that swamp. I have never told anyone about my swap friend. And on certain nights when I looked out my bedroom window, I can still hear his lonesome cry. And I know it is no fun being alone in life.

Midnight journey

Why me, was my faint cry. I was afraid to raise my voice too loud.

Why afraid?

I should yell for help.

Demand help.

Somehow I understood this was a special mission. The Angels began to lead me by the hand. We go through the house and I've passed my parents' bedroom door. Isn't it funny, they don't look like my parents when they are sleeping.

The brilliant glow from the angel lights up the entire hallway. I wonder if the angel is a boy or girl. The light is so strong I can't even make out its face. Not a word has been spoken between us. I had been awakened by a gentle nudge on my shoulder.

The angel had extended its hand and I took it by instinct and followed her. A peaceful and warm feeling goes through my body. Somehow I knew, I would never experience anything quite like this again. Why me, why me echoed through my brain. Was this real? I wasn't afraid. I felt safe, the safest I had ever felt in my life.

It took me through the front door. We walked right through the door. It unfolded its white wings and it gently lifted me off the ground. We were flying. I felt as if my whole body was lighter than air. A great happy feeling raced through my body. All I could see was my hand and a mist of white light. We flew, no we drifted, higher and higher into the moonlit sky.

Birds were flying past us and they were all singing to us. Their voices were a sweet melody. I began to sing with them. I dance in the air with them. There were hundreds or thousands of little birds singing. Are they trying to tell me something?

In front of me are rainbows, they are filled with every color imaginable. I waved goodbye to the birds as we enter a soft gentle cloud. A melody of flutes came from the clouds. A Golden door opens to let us in. In front of me there is a road made out of silver sparkling diamonds.

I am taking the high road with an angel as my guide. Actually it was more like floating. Flowers sit along the roadside. They are the largest flowers than I have ever seen. I see great wonderful flowers, exotic flowers, kinds that I have never seen before. Some of the flowers are blue and red. Some of them even have stripes. There are some polka dot flowers. Even the flowers are dancing and singing. One of them reaches out and shakes my hand. Another flower gives me a gentle kiss.

Some of the flowers picked me up and then let me gently down. This is a great adventure. They are blowing clouds of multi-colored smoke. They smell so very sweet. Each step makes me happy and a little tired. But best of all, I have a feeling of peace inside. I have a feeling, that can never be duplicated.

The flowers fade out of sight in the air becomes thick. It is as if I am in a fog. How long have I been gone? Will I ever return? Do I really want to go home? The road on my journey begins to move like a conveyor belt. It moves me along. Funny looking trees dot the side of the road.

Some of the flowers have faces of my friends. They smile at me and tell me to be brave. Others tell me that they love me. One tree has the face of my mom and dad waving goodbye. I notice a small tear in their eyes. Don't worry, I yelled, I'll be all right. Some of the trees have pieces of my life hanging on the branches. We are beginning to slow down. The angel let's go of my hand. I knew that from now on I was on my own.

A huge gate at the top of the hill stands before me. I cannot see over it. Its bars are made of red and white roses. I can hear a beckoning music from the inside the gate.

The gate begins to open, soothing voices are calling. Come to me.

Knife

I'm not really sure what happened. One minute I'm walking, the next I'm lying on the ground. The ground is hard, wet and cold and a knife is sticking out of my side. The pain is searing. Red blood is coming out. I watched myself die. I hate nightmares like this one. My side actually hurts. It all seemed so real.

Sweat pores from my head as I stumble out of my bed. Golden sunlight is burning through the window, I stretch, but my side still hurts, I check the mirror to see if I am still there. Trembling I hold onto my dresser to calm my nerves. My legs are wobbly. They don't want to hold me. Why does this one dream keep haunting me? Is it trying to tell me something?

I can't shake the dream from my mind. I've got to get out of the house. Get some fresh air. Try to get the cobwebs out of my head. Have to think clearly. I'm too rational for this kind of stuff.

I'm walking down the alley, minding my own business, when I see a shiny bright light from a sharp piece of metal. My eyes are fixated on that knife.

No.

My brain screams. All I can see is a gloved covered hand holding a long shiny knife. It is heading towards me. I turn and begin to run. Heart beating out of control, I race as fast as I can. I can hear footsteps behind me, pounding on the ground.

I am running around corners, down streets of despair. Never can I run fast enough. In front of me is a wall of no return.

Trapped.

The knife of truth is only inches away. I should scream, do something. But I can't, facing life alone is too hard. The knife is breaking my skin of resistance.

Wake up.

Wake up. I can't. I find myself running. I am running from the knife of life. Will I ever stop running?

Masters voice

"Please hurry back."

I whine. I am so lonesome I could cry. They have left me alone. This house is big and I am afraid. I would like to watch television. A little music would be nice. They could have taken me. I told them I would be good.

How can they just decide to leave me like this? I almost start to cry. I think I hear a noise. Someone is coming toward the house. No doubt about it, I can hear footsteps. Should I call the police? I can't find the phone. Where is it? I was just playing with it yesterday.

Calm, I have to stay calm. This isn't easy, being quiet. I can hear them getting closer. Clank, it was just the postman. Thank goodness. I better put the mail on the table. I dropped one letter, I'll get it later.

I hope they never leave me home alone again. I can't handle the pressure. I'm not old enough to stay by myself, they should know that. Guess I'll get something to eat and drink some water.

I'll just have to wait on the couch. I could sleep, but I don't want to miss anything. I can hear a car in the driveway, it's about time. They are back. I am so happy to see them. I am proud to show them how brave I was.

The Miracle

It was a miracle that I met my wife. I had always felt God sent her to me. If nothing else I was a lucky man. Imagine my joy when I learned we would have a baby. I am at her side clutching her hand.

I know that this is a special moment in my life. It is one thing to be a husband; it is another to be a father. I prayed that I was up to the challenge. I wish I could absorb her pain. I am unable to speak. A lifetime flashes in front of my eyes. I am so excited, I am shaking.

"I love you." I whisper.

I hope that it will be over soon. Nine months. The waiting seems to have been a lifetime. Our love will now have a deeper meaning. Our marriage will have a special purpose. My throat is so dry. I can hardly breathe.

They are taking her to the delivery room. My heart is going crazy. Here comes the hard part I tell myself, just sitting, waiting, and worrying. Time seems like an eternity.

Please let them both be okay.

A nurse walks in the room. "Follow me," she says. I want to scream with pride. Lying next to my wife is a tiny miracle.

I pick up my daughter up with great care. I want to make sure I don't break her. What a precious beautiful baby. I can't believe it, I'm a dad. I cry with happiness as I pick Marsha up. Miracles still happen.

Flood

I was doing what the queen told me. How did I get myself in such a mess? Before I knew it I was caught in the rain; pouring in a steady stream. Will it ever quit falling? I know that I will be in trouble if the rain doesn't stop. I can't turn back. Don't want to make the queen angry.

I might be caught in a flood. It doesn't seem it wants to stop. It has rained hard before, but it has always stopped in time. The fear inside me rises. It doesn't look like the rain will ever stop, that makes things even scarier. The water is at the crest. It won't be much longer now. A wall of water sweeps me off my feet. I struggle to swim.

Harry turns off the bathtub.

"Harry, it's an ant."

I swim to the side of tube and make it back to my ant hill. I never did find any food.

The fire inside me

If only humans never stop to question things. The power of the mind is unbelievable. I am never quite succeeding at anything, never reaching my dreams. I am always trying, but not hard enough.

I want to be what they expect of me. I can only do my best. But I guess it isn't enough. I try to ignore their taunts. It isn't easy ignoring them. Please accept me as I am. I haven't turned out that bad.

I wish that I could make my dad proud of me. I have a sad feeling. I will never be good enough for him. I have a feeling I will never be great. I want to be free of my doubts.

In his been 20 years since my dad passed away. But I still have those feelings of not being good enough. Knowing that I never made him proud of me hurts. Feeling like I had let him down.

There are things I meant to say. Things I should have said. I hope I can still become what he wanted. I am still trying. Please let the fires inside me always burn brightly.

The wind blows

The wind blows over the mountains. It is an awesome force. It makes the trees wave to those who are passing by. On the wings of the wind you can hear the melody and morning birds. In the distance there is a rippling stream.

The torn shutter rattles against the lowly shack. I am back, the wind whisperers. I am ready, a broken down man. Waiting to be carried away, by the wind, it swirls around me and tries to pick me up.

The wind and I are together. I climbed the greatest heights. Travel to the distant lands. This is my destiny, blowing away into eternity.

I hear the voice

"David, it is your time." "Already, I haven't done anything worthwhile yet. I've done a lot of small things, but nothing really great." "You had your chance."

"May I go back," I pleaded.

"I will try harder. I can do some good. If you wait and see, I will prove it."

"It's been 36 years. I don't know if I should give you any more time."

"Give me more time, if not for me, for those who are like me. Maybe if I'm lucky, I can change their lives. If I try hard enough, I might be to help them out."

"You are now on borrowed time."

"Yes, I know time is precious. I realize that now. I will start this very minute. Not only that but I will never give up. I must make the world listen. It is so important."

The future of many people depends on me. I wonder how one person can make a difference. I have to try. I must hurry so I don't miss anyone. I must make good use of my time.

The island

Quiet, hush, do you hear it? There is that sound again. Be still my heart, so I can listen. I strain to hear the sound, it is fading away. I must continue this journey. No telling how long it will take me. Will I ever be home again?

This island is so large; I may never be able to explore all of it. Not sure that I want to. It is very hot out and the air is dry but I must continue. In front of me is another hill, I sigh. How many hills have I climbed? Some of them seem like mountains. At least I can now see the sandy shore.

It is closer. Must keep going, have to continue, I think to myself. Suddenly the sky turns a deep purple black. I am trembling inside, the sky lightens up again. I breathe a sigh of relief.

I must hurry. There may not be much time left. Should I put down what I am carrying? It is getting heavy, almost too heavy to carry alone. The others are depending on me. The queen has trusted me to deliver.

Keep going I can do it. It is a matter of mind over matter. The sand between my toes is hot and the water looks so refreshing. You can stop sun, go behind a cloud if you want to.

Wait till they see the food I am bringing. The water sure looks cool. I'm almost there just a little farther. I put the tray next to my wife. The kids are swimming in the lake.

"What took you so long?" my wife asked.

"The line was long."

"You forgot my potato chips."

"I'll be back."

Here I go again, walking another island. Will I ever be able to rest?

My shadow

He is my best friend. He never doubts me. One thing I like about him is that he always helps me to pretend.

"Hello," I tell him.

Did I really do that?

"It wasn't me," I tell my mom.

"I suppose you are going to tell me it was your shadow again."

Well, I was going to tell her that. It sounds like she isn't going to believe me. It does sound silly. How can I make her believe that it was my shadow?

I must remain calm. I can't expect adults to understand, not even my mom.

She tells me to clean up my mess and leaves the room.

"Okay shadow, it is time, we must act quickly."

Slowly I open the closet door. I hope it doesn't make any noise. We are on a secret mission. No one is watching. Yes, my magic kingdom is waiting.

"Shadow, are you ready? Close your eyes." We fade into a magical world.

My shadow is next to me.

"Did you see that giant candy bar?" He shakes his head. I wish he would talk to me. I get awful lonely at times. It is nice to have him with me, but it would be better if he talked to me.

The candy bar must be two hundred feet tall. Thousands of candy canes cover the ground. I look into the skies. There are giant marshmallow clouds hanging low enough to eat. I am tempted to take a bite. On the hill in front of me is a castle made out of cakes. The windows are made out of pink icing.

The skies above are with filled with cotton candy. My shadow is holding my hand. It is having as much fun as I am. I walk up to the king of the castle.

"Your honor, I would like a lot of treats."

"Take all you want."

The shadow and I play games all day. I can see that it is time for us to return. With a smile a mile wide, I climb back into my closet. I open the door and start dreaming.

I know whenever I want company or have fun; all I have to do is open my closet door.

The civil war

Screams echo through the air. They are louder than ever. Screams are so loud that they penetrate through my spine. I shivered. I clutched my sisters and brothers close to me. Tears are rushing down my cheeks.

"Mommy," I cried inside.

I wish I can find a way to help them. And only if I were bigger I would show those white folks. Anger fills my heart. Why are they fighting? A loud shriek fills the air. I hope that it will be over soon.

Finally a deadly silence fills the air. Shrieks quit and my dad enters the shack. His shirt is torn to shreds. Blood and skin sticks to his clothing. His face is sweating. I think he is trying to hide a tear.

We huddled together in our two room shack, trying to comfort each other.

"Children, I would like to talk to you. Whatever you do, don't forget this day. Never fill your hearts with hate. We need to prove to the white people that we do deserve freedom. We can fight back with strength and positive actions. We need to show them how great we can be."

It has been 20 years since that special night. Dad died,

the beatings were too much. But I will never forget his words. If he could see me now, I think to myself. I have my own little farm. I am free. Every since the war, I have struggled to better myself.

Dad, I cry as I face the militant sky, it hasn't been easy, but I am free. I miss you but I look up to you. I am proud as I lay kneeling on the ground, that your dreams for me, have come true. Somehow I know the battle for equality and freedom will never be over.

Deer

I am not against hunting. But I must say that deer are special creatures. The air whistles around my head. The soft whisper of the wind races through the tall pine trees in the distance.

I am taking a walk through Black Lake Woods. I could hear the footsteps, and I wondered which way I should go. How had I been separated from the rest of the group? Quickly, I must go, quickly. They may be looking for me.

On a hill far away I see my friends and they don't see me. Still I know that they are not far away. My friends disappear out of sight. I must run. Run as fast as I can. The woods are so thick, I may become lost. I try to run faster but the ground is too uneven. Struggling to catch my breath, I begin to walk.

Without warning a deer appears in front of me. A slight frost fills the air. The deer doesn't seem to be startled. It acts as if it wants me to follow it. It walks a little and then stops. Sometimes in life, you just have to trust someone.

Step by step we are like partners in a strange dance. I waltz with my mind and it swings through the trees. When I turn my head, I spot our campsite. When I look back, the deer has vanished.

Abandoned

To be truthful I never expected it to happen to me. It's embarrassing when you think about it. I find myself along the side of the road, hoping that someone will help me, it is starting to get dark out and I'm afraid.

It has turned really cold and there are not any streetlights here. Just like that, on the spur of the moment, I had been abandoned. Why does everyone pass me by? Can't they see I need help? There are a lot of bright lights on the highway, but no one seems intent on stopping.

Everyone keeps passing me by. Apparently they can't hear me yell, stop. My cries go unheard. No one is listening. If it wasn't for bad luck, I could go on, on my own. I am so tired, and I feel all alone. As if no one really cares.

I did everything they asked me. This isn't my fault. They neglected me. I tried to warn them, but they were too busy listening to the radio. Look what has happened. I was left on a lonely highway to fend for myself. It just isn't fair.

Maybe they'll change their minds and come back for me. I can't believe how dark it has become. Have no light to comfort me. In the distance I can hear the roar of engines. Maybe it is them. Hopefully they have had a change of mind.

The car is slowing down. It is stopping and they haven't forgotten me. My engine jumps with joy. Then they begin to put gas into my tank. I'm glad they came back I have been a faithful car. With my engine humming, I drive home, and park in my safe comfortable garage.

Love is a triangle

A day that so calm, that I call it ordinary. Fading personalities are reaching for eternal flames. This I will do, as their two souls begin to converse and they become one.

A special music fills the air, floating on the land of love. I can even hear birds singing in the trees.

I've begin to cast away the past, hoping that I will be happy in the future. I conquer all my wonderful dreams. They realize they must face difficulties together.

I will love her for all my tomorrows and my love for her will never end. It is a true love. A love that is beyond comprehension. Save the last dance for me. Our love can be always free.

Love can become the guiding force of our marriage. I don't care about reality. We can push it away. In the darkest storm, through the fiercest pain, in every moment of life, love can make a difference.

Yes, love can be a triangle. It will never fail it.

Almost a perfect marriage

A soft voice speaks in the night.

"David, I'm afraid."

"Move closer."

We are facing the unknown together. There is no "I" in our marriage. We try to work out differences without treading on our individual personalities. It isn't healthy to agree on everything.

"Do you remember when our first child was born?" I asked.

A gleam of maternal pride enters her eyes.

"Yes," she whispers, "how can I forget."

We are two lives sailing the seas of life to together. After several years together, we are still looking for the stars. We are spending special moments together. I often think I have a lot of knowledge, but it doesn't compare to my wife's inner strength, her calmness, her sense of fairness.

I find myself praying for good things for my children. I know that I can't protect them from life, as much as I would like too. When my wife becomes ill, I wish I could take on her illness.

Although I try to be a good husband, I am always striving to do a lot better. Love helps us survive through the good and bad times. Hope is eternal. We work toward our goals as one ship. We respect each other.

Yes, you have my promise. We will be together through strife and good times. It isn't a perfect marriage because we are human. But at least we try. I promise I will do everything I can in her battle with bone cancer.

The shadow stalks

There it is again. Hanging around, waiting to tease me. Did you happen to see it? Look closely. There it is again.

"Quiet," I said to my friend.

He ignores my request. No matter how hard I try I can't seem to lose him. There he goes, laughing again. I think that we will play tag for a while. He will never be able to catch me. No matter how fast I run, he keeps up with me. Resting, I sit on the school swings. My older brother is with me.

"Let us hide," I yell.

Quickly we run to a tall true tree and hide underneath it. It offers a lot of shade from the warm hot summer sun. The heat is unbearable and we sit laughing and telling each other stories.

"I think we lost him," Jim says.

We both laugh at how clever we are. We keep looking at the playground and wonder if he is lurking somewhere. Perhaps he is hiding in the doorway.

"You might be right," I agreed with Jim, "But somehow I doubt it."

Why is he following us? Perhaps we should stay under this tree. It is awful hot today. Other children are taking off their shirts but, I never go without a shirt. Jim is my only friend and even he and I are starting to drift apart.

I don't want to grow up if it means becoming like Jim. He doesn't seem to have much fun anymore. He takes everything way too serious.

Overhead a kite is dancing in the air, orchestrated by the music of the wind. Somehow I know, that our days of having fun together are numbered. Jim is three years older than me and he acts a lot older. I don't want to lose the only friend I have.

We can hear the laughter of other children playing on the school grounds.

"Let's make a run for it," I said.

He began to run. I followed Jim. It was following us again. My heart was pounding loudly. Jim was close by my side, but he can run a lot faster than I can. Faster, we have to run faster. I spotted an empty house at the edge of the school ground.

"Let's rest over there," I panted.

We race to the side of the house, laughing and straining

to catch our breath.

"He'll never find us here."

"I wouldn't be so sure," Jim said.

We listened, but we couldn't hear him. I knew it was getting late. I decided it was now or never. I yelled as I dashed out of cover. There he was, right behind us. I tried every trick I could, but I couldn't seem to lose him. We ran all over the school ground, zigzagging, jumping and leaping and nothing worked.

It was starting to get dark and I knew that our shadows were done playing for today. I knew I would be back tomorrow the play with my shadow; the question was, how many more times will I be able to get Jim to join me?

Make-believe

I am alone at last. Believe it or not, I like to be alone. I don't need anyone. I can hear him screaming in the background. My parents are at it again. It seems like they are always arguing. That's all they do anymore. Why did they ever get married?

Anger races through my body. Stop. Stop, I yell inside. It's always the same thing, day in and day out. Sometimes I wish had never been born. I close my eyes.

My soul begins to drift away as I've become alive in a different world. The room in front of me begins to spin. It spins faster and faster. Colors spin around in my head and they are dancing with wonderful dreams.

A soft hum vibrates through my brain. It is taking me away into a make-believe Valley. They will never find me here. I don't care if I ever come back. I love coming to this place. It is always calm and pretty. There are sunbeam flowers reaching into the sky. They are here just for my enjoyment.

Music begins to fill the air. And I can see the grass around me dancing. A chipmunk is sitting on my shoulder. All the animals are my friends. I have no enemies, no cares or worries. I can't hear my parents here. They are far away.

I am at peace. For once in life, I am surrounded by love and kindness. Their yelling had stopped. They were calling my name, looking for me. It is time to eat. I'm not going back. They can look all they want.

I know if I return, they will start fighting again. I can live in my make believe land forever. I am wanted here.

"David, David," they keep calling my name, but they can't find me. I hope they never find me. They quit looking and start arguing again. I'm glad I have someplace to hide. They can look all they want, but they never will find me.

Trapped

Often we are trapped in the cobwebs of our mind. When I was a young boy I was very naive, part of it was because of my age. A lot of it was because of my sheltered life. My world consisted of about one square mile around my house.

The farthest I had ever been was to my elementary school. Compared to the old looking neighborhood I was growing up in, it looked very modern. It was one story high and made out of shiny red bricks. Only in school was I able to get a small taste of the world. And reading about the world and seeing and living in it are different animals.

It is no wonder I would fear almost everything. Lying in bed I noticed that the roof was starting to cave in. One would think that I would yell for help. I didn't. I was afraid that no one would believe me.

Not that I blame them. There has been an occasion or two where I panicked over nothing. I had read the story about the boy who had cried wolf. This is for real. I can see the ceiling bulging.

I should run, leave my bedroom, but I'm frozen in hot fear. My heart is pushing blood through my brain so fast I can't seem to think straight.

Or if my roof falls, I will never be able to see my friends or parents again. Even my dreams can't save me from the truth of reality. Flashes of times we spent together race through my brain. They have been good times, times that I will never forget.

If I get out of this I'll show them that I do care. I will try harder in school and try to behave. It is getting dark. It is only inches from my face. It may be too late to call for help. I can't hold on much longer. I can hear footsteps. Help is on the way. I will be saved.

I can hear my parents calling my name.

"I'm here," comes my muffled reply.

They yank the cover off my face. My mom hugs me. I know that it was a cheap trick, but it worked. They are paying a lot more attention to me. All I wanted was to be loved.

Forbidden mission

I had been a special agent for the government. I had promised myself that I was giving it all up. I have found a regular job and I like the stability.

Hopefully this will be my last mission. I can barely see the car lights on the distant hill. It took me several months of hard work, but I have found their meeting place. The hard part is to find out what they are up to.

It all started with a phone call eight weeks ago. It was from the president of United States. He even called me Mr. Bell. He told me they needed my help. I still don't quite understand why had picked me. I had told everyone who would listen; I wanted to retire from being a secret agent. Although I knew it must be important, but I never had a hard assignment.

A lot must be at stake. They even gave me a gun, even if I don't know how to use it. They warned me not to tell anyone, not even my family about the mission. I couldn't tell anybody until the mission was over.

If my wife found out I was here watching spies, instead of working, she would be very upset. I don't like keeping secrets from her. I had promised her that I was quitting my old profession. Still, how can you tell the president no?

I'm only a few feet away from the cabin. The flash of light catches my attention from the window. There are two more quick flashes of light. I will never find out what they're doing from here. I have to get closer. I wish I had worn a heavier coat. It is getting colder outside.

It is so cold out, I'm not sure if I can stay out here much longer. Quietly, I make my way under the moonlight to the shack.

Perhaps I am walking to my own death. Accidentally I step on a twig and I freeze in my tracks. Hopefully no one heard me.

No one seems to have heard me. I sigh in relief. The window is only a few feet away. Rubbing my hands together for warmth, I had finally made it to the outside walls of the shack. I am shivering as I struggle to hear conversation from the inside. I can make out at least four different voices.

Bombs, I had heard the word bombs and I was terrified. Innocent people's lives were at stake. They were going to terrorize a school. Then I heard the voices say Sedalia elementary school. And I'm worried to death.

A lump forms in my throat. I am really scared. They are

planning to bomb the school that I have been volunteering in. Now I know why the president had chosen me. I get back to my car as fast as I can. I mustn't tell anyone, those were my orders. The president doesn't want this group to get too much attention.

I look everywhere I could, but I don't see any bombs. I tried to act like everything is normal. Don't panic the kids, I thought. I was filled with fear, I can't find any bombs.

That night after my wife was asleep, I left my house. I looked around the school and still couldn't see any bombs. I was hiding behind a bush when I see the same car I had seen at the tiny shack.

The ravine, they were putting the bombs in the creek near the school. Of course, I thought. No one ever goes there. There are enough bombs to blow up the whole neighborhood. I must act now, I thought.

"All right, hold it." Then I fired two shots. Just to make sure. I use my walkie-talkie to call the FBI.

In school the next day I acted like everything was the same. The children said hi, never realizing that I was a hero.

The repair shop

I have kept my secret for years. I've been acting like a regular family man. They are all asleep now. I lift up the rug in my kitchen. My family doesn't suspect I have a secret repair shop underneath my kitchen floor.

And I must get busy. I should tell them that I'm not sure they would understand. I have to be quiet. My wife is a light sleeper. My special welding machine is very busy. This is the 10th one this week. I can't keep up such a fast pace. Old age is creeping up on me.

Ring, ring, my translator is getting a call.

"How is everything coming?"

"Okay," I answer, "but I'm afraid we are going to be discovered some day."

"Yes we know."

I am almost finished, only need a little more time. It won't be long until we have the rest of our population here. I can't help but wonder how much time is left. Not much, our planet is dying quickly.

The voice faded away. I knew that our planet was

dying. I had transported most of our population, but there are still many behind. I am done for the night. Quickly I get into bed.

"Did you know that some people think they have seen aliens? Imagine," my wife said.

Aliens, I thought to myself. If only she knew. We are almost like them. Why can't the earthlings accept our kind? I was the first one here, so I could build a transmitter to bring my fellow aliens to Earth.

I drifted off to sleep dreaming of my days on my home planet. Humans don't know how good they have it. I hope they don't ruin their planet like we destroyed ours.

After watching all these movies, I'm not sure that we will ever be welcomed on this planet. I don't understand why they can't welcome us like long-lost brothers.

Peace love

This is an eerie dark blue sky. Not even the moon is out tonight. The streak of lightning, lights up the sky for a few brief seconds. Thick distant trees reach toward the clouds, it tries, but it can't stretch far enough. I am standing here trying to remain calm.

It must be closed by. It was only a few days ago when I first spotted it. I saw it ride across the southern field of my farm. It hovered for a few seconds and then flew off.

It looked like a giant dish, I was afraid to call it a UFO. I didn't want people to think I was crazy. Another bolt of lightning strikes in the sky. I hear a loud crack. The wind is starting to get a lot stronger.

In the distance I could see a large cloud of dust. An eerie reddish hue is right over a distant hill. A soft whirling sound fills the air. It is getting closer and closer.

It -- is over the hill jumping up and down. My God and I thought to myself, it must be at least 400 feet wide. It looks like it has tiny windows in the side. The noise is getting louder and louder.

Something, a container is coming out of one of the

Windows. The spaceship stops in midair. The noise becomes louder and louder.

A white container floats to the ground. With a flash the flying saucer is gone. I still can't believe my eyes dropped. I opened the metal container and there is a letter inside of it. I tremble as I open it. A very special warmth fills my body as I read it. It only contains two words.

Peace Love

The secret will be mine. I don't know if the world is ready for such a message. Will the world ever be ready?

Stowaway

I had done it. I had made a lot of plans and was well prepared. It took me a lot of nerve to go through with my plans. I am hidden on a rocket to the moon. I will be the first stowaway. I will be famous.

I can hear the astronauts on the other side of the wall talking. I am hidden in a side chamber. Nobody knows that I am in here. I hope I brought plenty of food. It is getting cramped in here, but I can do it.

How much time, I thought. It won't be long before takeoff. Then a roar fills the air. The rocket begins to shake. We are moving. At first we start off slowly, climbing, we go faster and faster. I think about my family below. I hope they understand. This wasn't an easy decision. But my life wasn't going anywhere. I figure the headlines will give me a lot of job opportunities. I was tired of being out of work.

I miss my family. As we get higher I can see the Earth below. It is getting smaller and smaller. What a strange sight. I have done it. It won't be long before we land on the moon.

I can't wait. Objects start flying around us. Space

We are in space. Then I can see two eyes looking through the hole in the wall. I have been discovered. What will be my fate?

"George, the there is a spider in there."

"I wonder how he got in the hole."

He's a stowaway," one of them laughed. They don't care that I am on the spaceship. I sigh with relief. I am on my way. I will be the first spider in space.

Kings Island

I love driving. We have been planning this trip to King's Island for a long time. The countryside along 71 S. is beautiful. I especially liked looking at houses. There are so many different ones and beautiful ones.

Often my wife had to remind me to keep my eyes on the road. It's not that I'm a bad driver; I just like to notice things. Usually my children would warn me about my driving.

"Watched the road dad, I'm getting out if you don't watch where you're going."

Six o'clock in the morning is the best time to drive. It isn't really hot yet. The sun is just starting to come out.

"Looks like it's going to rain," my wife says.

"I don't care if it does. We're going to have a good time and rain will just make the place less crowded."

I was more excited than the kids. It was hard to concentrate on my driving. Almost there, I thought to myself.

"Look," I yelled.

We could see the miniature Eiffel tower to the left. I know it couldn't be much farther. My wife woke up the kids. We were one of the first cars in the parking lot. But already, even at seven o'clock the lines were starting to get long.

I was really impressed. We couldn't decide where to go first. I wanted everyone to calm down. I knew we would get to see all of it. We had all day. As we walked through the gate it started to pour down raining.

We bought raincoats. I decided we wouldn't let a little bit of rain ruin our fun. My wife and I just walked, watching the kids ride rides. Marsha and Pam were a lot more daring than our son Tony. They are only a year apart with Marsha being the oldest and Tony the youngest. The rain lasted only long enough to keep the place from getting crowded.

My grandson wanted me to ride with him. His ruse was that he was scared. I kept saying my prayers on our way to the top. It was my first and last ride. To be truthful, I don't understand why people think getting the living daylights scared out of you is fun, not me; I'm a walk around kind of guy. I'm a people watcher, not crazy.

I did like the ride called "it's a small world." my kids were upset that I rode it three times. It was a slow ride, just my speed. I also like the antique cars, although my wife insisted on driving. It was payback for not paying attention to the road on the way down here.

Just before dark, sky divers landed in the square. My girls were just entering their teen years and just had to have autographs. The day was finished by climbing to the top of the miniature Eifel tower and watching fireworks.

At first I resisted a trip to Kings Island. All in all I had a great time and I'm glad that we went.

The last time

The last time I saw your face, you were standing on the corner. You were acting coy, as if you didn't know me. I can't seem to forget you.

The last time I heard your voice, it was like a gentle breeze. Like wind chimes it echoed through my brain into my heart. I was entranced by your eyes and I never understood a word you said. Was it only yesterday I heard your voice? It seems like an eternity.

I can't think straight.

I didn't know that it might be the last time. I look at the bottom of the ravine and my tears begin. There is nothing but ashes left. I can still taste our last kiss.

I get in my car, back up and then head forward to the cliff. This will be the last time. Or will it?

My shadow cries

Often my shadow cries, but not I. my eyes are dry. Tears of loneliness fill my broken heart, but my pain to my shadow I chart. You see the haunting, but not of me. It is my shadow that can't be free.

Follow me and take away my pain. I can't lose you; you come back again and again. But atlas it is my shadow that suffers not me. The sad truth is clear, my shadow and I are the same my dear.

When darkness fades

Yes it was yesterday. Only yesterday, a thousand dreams away. My shadows and truth played a deadly game. No one calls my name. Going down in flames?

It was only yesterday that I played. Just back then, I was only ten. Seems like ages ago, I know. Oh yesterday, the memory easily fade.

Now I'm afraid to play. Afraid of what they may say. I have childhood dreams and schemes no longer able to return. Oh to be younger, I do so year. Flames of years slowly burn, driving to deaths' brink.

Ten to seventy years old. Seventy to ten years old, if only I could return once again. Circles of life, love and dreams and so many things between. Day and night, night and day and I find myself ten again and at play. And the darkness fades.

The night stalks, campfires

Blazing fires, flames leaping to the sky. Never ever to die, my memories are over hot coals. Swamp fire all aglow. Shine on heaven and forever glow. On the edge on the swamp I lay, afraid to move, afraid to die.

The heat is easing, from the flames and the hot summer night.

Another explosion, a burst of bright light.

Through the mud, sublime, on my stomach I crawl. Swamp fire creatures surround me. I can hear their footsteps. I must find a way to escape. A wolf is nearby, I take my time. Finally I reach my car. The sky is a bright orange from the moon. Another night of research is over.

Angel in the morning

An angel in the morning came without any warning. It sings to the new morning. This angel of the morning is calling me. Will I be joining this angel? I look out my window and see a second angel.

There's an angel on my shoulder. If you listen close enough, you can hear it. Its image is very clear. You never really understand why the sun comes up or why it is morning. How many years? How many tears? Yet life keeps on going.

Is there a land of eternity? If so, does it wait for me? One thing I can be sure of, if I keep my faith, an Angel will always be looking over me.

Dragonfly

And here he cried, seeping through the swamp. The cry crawls to the creatures of the lily pad. There it goes again, raising its ugly head, giving his way back toward some type of safety.

As he walks, the trees moved their leaves out of the way. They bow in his presence. A few birds interrupt his cries. They are creatures of temptation. I am trying to pretend that everything is normal. He knows better, after all this isn't a city, it is a dirty hot swamp. He clings to what reality he can.

Who will ever believe I love a dragonfly? It had a greenish black body with paper thin wings. It seemed to perch instead of sitting. It looked like it was ready to attack, when he turned and started to head back.

He feared that he would be mistaken for an insect and be eaten alive. The man wondered, why the swamp didn't seem to notice the strange creature. Donald sits in his crowded small tent. He is almost shaking inside. He wishes that he had brought a larger tent. He sits on the thin blue cot and watches as a fly torments him. The heat is stifling. Not one whiff of a breeze is anywhere.

Unknown sounds drift back and forth. The skies are starting to turn a deadly black. He looks out the opening in his tent and realizes a storm is brewing. It is too late to run. He'll have to stick it out.

The sun is covered by ominous dark clouds. A storm is playing in the sky and he wonders when it will pass. The storm is not an unusual event for this swamp. As he watches me, I notice that the dragonfly is flying about lazily. It is trying in vain to out fly the oncoming storm.

A sudden bolt of light, a loud crackling hiss and a smell of burning is in the air. Stand still, the dragonfly flutters its wings and returns to the ground. An interruption, a volcanic seizures rumble through its body.

Bewildered, the man walks around his tent as if in a trance. He has decided not to reveal to anyone what he has seen. He knows that the dragonfly belongs to the swamp. Besides, no one would believe him anyway.

The lighthouse

Hope my boat rocks no more. As I viewed the lighthouse on the shore, will we travel for evermore? I would like to think that I travel to the welcome mat at the door. I have spent many nights sailing on the sea. There are too many days for me to be on the sea.

Sometimes in life we travel our path, faithful and true. When we reach our destiny, we need to leave our complaints behind. Yellow gold is the treasure of the ship. The Asian island is left behind.

I will never know who might love me. I struck gold on a moonless night. The gold is now mine. Yes we have left the island out of sight. We are six men at sea. We have done a wicked deed.

I will live my life in luxury. Why should I split my gold? I am starting to think of a plan. A gleam enters my mind. It is an evil plan, but the bounty will be mine.

Asleep

They are all asleep. It is time to implement my plan. I have to be quiet, quiet as I can be. I take two steps then pause. Slowly I put my gold on a rowboat. I start rowing away from the boat. For some reason the air is getting colder.

I must be patient; I can see the lighthouse in the distance. I'll be there soon, and I'll be rich too. The boat is almost out of sight and I am rowing as hard as I can. I will be rich. My feet are getting wet. I look down and notice that my rowboat has a hole in the bottom.

I am rowing as fast as I can. The sea is winning. My heart skips a beat. I have to do something. I begin throwing some of the gold over the side. My boat is sinking. I gather the remaining gold in my arms. The lighthouse is almost within reach. I can see the faces of those I left behind in its doorway. As I began to sink below the water, I can hear their chilling laughter.

I hear their laughter one final time.

Tainted love

Was it only yesterday? It seems like a lot longer to me. Can't be, it must be at least an eternity. My heart still pounds wildly. True it was just a brief encounter. It was only a split second and then she was gone. I was nnly a few minutes at the most, but enough time to convince me she was special.

Who can forget that face? She had a sweet innocent face, penetrating hazel brown eyes and full cherry lips. Yes it was love, instant love. I consider it everlasting love. My feet never would touch the ground. I was afraid to look back and she walked by. I was afraid to speak; silently I said I love you.

The moon is out and I walked nervously up and down the same street. I keep hoping she will come this way again. She is part of my dreams. If I see her, I hope I have the carriage to speak. Even if I just say hello to her.

Here she comes, lovelier than ever. She is so beautiful I can't even move. I am frozen in my tracks. She is getting closer and closer. Speak my heart, try to be brave. She is within a few feet of me. She walks right past me and I haven't said a word. Maybe when she comes tomorrow I will have the nerve to say something.

Two years have gone by. Each night I walked that street

hoping against hope that she will notice me. Even if she would just smile at me, I don't think that asking too much.

She is getting closer and I mouth the words, I love you. She has such a beautiful face and lovely soft hair. I have come to the conclusion, that humans just don't like ghosts.

The last dance

Save the last dance for me.

Oh twisted destiny
Why can't she see
There is a person inside me
I just want to be free
Music fades in and out
Wait for me, I shout
The lights begin to fade
The music turns to a whisper
Across the floor glides
A swan princess with golden hair
With one great swoop
We become one and dance
I'm afraid to hold her too close
Afraid that she might break
For a sliver of a lifetime
I am happy
And had joined the dance of life
Will it be my last dance?

The shack in the meadow

One day a unicorn crosses the meadow on his tip toes. With a whisper in his voice and a twinkle in his eye the unicorn hides under the tallest tree. A smile crosses his face as he stopped to rest.

He wiped the dust off his tunic. His high black boots shine in the summer light; they shine through the tallest trees. He is on a special mission, looking for one lost boy who needs help.

He listens to the wind and hears a faint cry. He begins to dance across the meadow. The cry is getting louder. At the edge of the meadow sits a lonely shack. In the corner, dad is working away. A young boy is in the bedroom dreaming about a friend.

The unicorn and the boy began to play. He knows that he will have to leave the boy someday, but for today they are friends. As the boy falls asleep, the unicorn has one promised he will keep, I will do my very best to make some child happy.

Misty eye rain

I listened to the falling rain. I listen to pitter patter, such happy dancing chatter. Tab dancing on my window pane. Oh how I love to listen to the rain.

As young boy, it helps me to dream again, drown out the pain. Love and laughter what a wonderful game life is. The rain even knows my name.

The tears of heaven fall into my garden and they help my dreams grow. I raise my tulip lips to drink the sweet nectar. I smell the orange lemonade of my fruited imagination. I like playing silly games.

I listen at my door for tales of forgotten lore. I'm lying on the beach of a sandy shore. That is what dreams are for. I listen to the rain; it is calling my name, pretend and be happy again.

As I turn pages of life

As you turn the pages of life, there are many stories unexpected. Things never turn out like you had imagined. A lot of things were harder than you expected. But through it all we keep turning the pages, hoping for the best.

Our book of life is never complete until the final page. We never know what words will be written on the next page. One thing that we do learn, nothing is as bad as it seems when it happens.

So I keep turning my pages, writing down my thoughts, living life the best I can. When you think about it, that's all anyone can do.

Made in the USA
Middletown, DE
13 August 2018